WORDS FAIL ME SOMETIMES.

This may come as a surprise to you, holding this book, because you've probably seen *Hamilton*, for which I composed roughly 27,000 words to be performed over the course of two hours and 45 minutes. But the book you hold in your hands is a celebration of the point where words fail and the other elements take over and create something new.

Musical theater isn't an art form. It's 14 art forms smashed together. And when they coalesce in exactly the right way, I believe it is more powerful than pretty much everything. This book celebrates the art forms in *Hamilton* that transform it from words on a page and breathe it to life. Every stitch in Paul Tazewell's dazzling, 18th-century-in-Technicolor costumes. Howell Binkley's unreal sculptures of light. Nevin Steinberg's subtle, expansive sound design that allows you to understand all 27,000 words in a soundscape entirely his own. David Korins' deceptively simple set that evokes both 18th-century shipbuilding and tips its hat to hip-hop (we got two turntables, y'all).

There is this incredible cast, who does the impossible, eight times a week: tells this story and makes it fresh for every new audience. Broadway casts are like chefs: last night's audience had their meal, and you've got to make it just as good every night, from scratch. For every actor you see on stage, there is a talented team of dressers and crew backstage, facilitating quick changes, moving desks at JUST the right moment, following our leads with spotlights—they are the unsung heroes of this enterprise.

Then there is the Cabinet, the three people who heard the first version of every song in this show and made them better. Andy Blankenbuehler's movement in this show carves out every lyric and manages an electric lyricism unlike any I've ever seen. Alex Lacamoire's orchestrations for our incredible band and string quartet make me question why I haven't been writing for strings this whole time. And then there is Thomas Kail, who marshalls and focuses all the disparate geniuses listed above, points us in the same direction, and keeps us smiling and having fun the whole time.

When I think about the contributions of this incredible team—the years they have sacrificed in pursuit of this idea, the man-hours they have spent prepping music, or rehearsing, or auditioning, or dancing in a basement—so that for two hours and 45 minutes, we can tell you the story of *Hamilton*…

Words fail me. Enjoy.

LIN-MANUEL MIRANDA

HOW DOES A BASTARD, ORPHAN, SON OF A WHORE AND A SCOTSMAN, DROPPED IN THE MIDDLE OF A FORGOTTEN SPOT IN THE CARIBBEAN BY PROVIDENCE, IMPOVERISHED, IN SQUALOR, GROW UP TO BE A HERO AND A SCHOLAR?

THE TEN-DOLLAR FOUNDING FATHER WITHOUT A FATHER GOT A LOT FARTHER BY WORKING A LOT HARDER, BY BEING A LOT SMARTER, BY BEING A SELF-STARTER, BY FOURTEEN, THEY PLACED HIM IN CHARGE OF A TRADING CHARTER. AND EVERY DAY WHILE SLAVES WERE BEING SLAUGHTERED OR CARTED AWAY ACROSS THE WAVES, HE STRUGGLED AND KEPT HIS GUARD UP. INSIDE, HE WAS LONGING FOR SOMETHING TO BE A PART OF, THE BROTHER WAS READY TO BEG, STEAL, BORROW OR BARTER

A L E

X A N

D E R

LIN-MANUEL MIRANDA

HEY YO,

I'M JUST
LIKE MY
COUNTRY,
I'M YOUNG,
SCRAPPY
AND
HUNGRY

AND I'M
NOT
THROWING
AWAY MY
SHOT.

HAM

LIN-MANUEL MIRANDA

ILTON

WE FOUGHT

WITH HIM . . .

WASH
WE ARE OUTGUNNED, OUTMANNED, OUTN

ME?

I TRUSTED

HIM.

CHRISTOPHER JACKSON

INGTON

BERED, OUTPLANNED. WE GOTTA MAKE AN ALL OUT STAND

ED HIM.

AND ME?

I'M THE DAMN FOOL THAT SHOT HIM.

BU

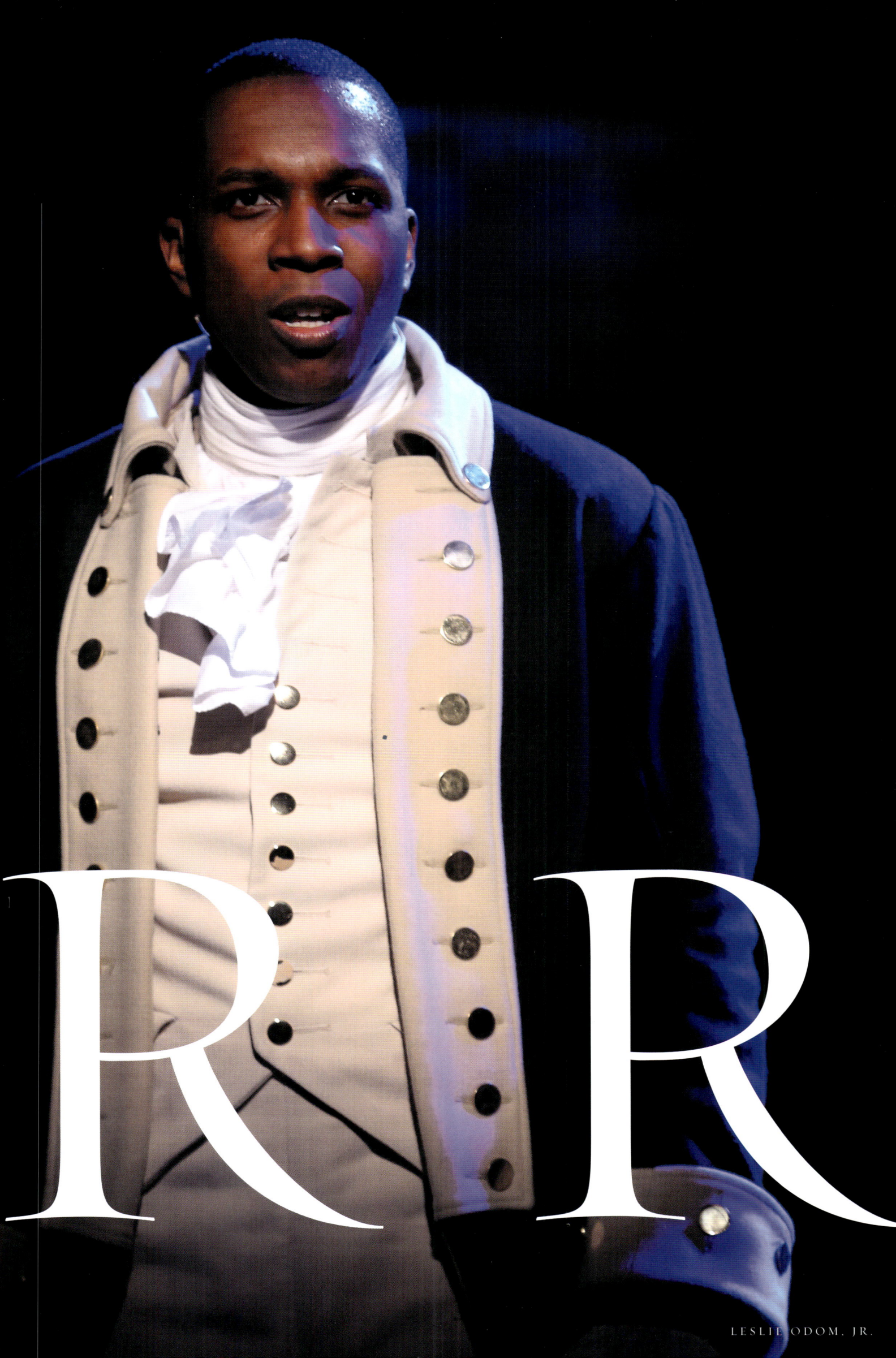

R R

LESLIE ODOM, JR.

IF WE WIN OUR INDEPENDENCE? 'ZAT A GUARANTEE OF FREEDOM AN ENDLESS CYCLE OF VENGEANCE AND DEATH WITH NO DEFEND BETWEEN ALL THE BLEEDIN' 'N FIGHTIN' I'VE BEEN READIN' 'N WRITIN'. OF STATES? WHAT'S THE STATE OF OUR NATION? I'M PAST ACTION'S AN ACT OF CREATION! I'M LAUGHIN' IN THE FACE OF CASUAL

FOR OUR DESCENDANTS? OR WILL THE BLOOD WE SHED BEGIN
ANTS? I KNOW THE ACTION IN THE STREET IS EXCITIN', BUT JESUS,
WE NEED TO HANDLE OUR FINANCIAL SITUATION. ARE WE A NATION
PATIENTLY WAITIN'. I'M PASSIONATELY SMASHIN' EVERY EXPECTATION, EVERY
TIES AND SORROW, FOR THE FIRST TIME, I'M THINKIN' PAST TOMORROW

S I S
T E R

RENÉE ELISE GOLDSBERRY

PHILLIPA SOO

LOOK AROUND, LOOK AROUND AT HOW LUCKY WE ARE TO BE ALIVE RIGHT NOW! HISTORY IS HAPPENING IN MANHATTAN AND WE JUST HAPPEN TO BE IN THE GREATEST CITY IN THE WORLD! CUZ I'VE BEEN READING COMMON *SENSE* BY THOMAS PAINE. SO MEN SAY THAT I'M INTENSE OR I'M INSANE.

THE REVOLUTION'S HAPPENING IN NEW YORK!

YOU WANT A REVOLUTION? I WANNA REVELATION SO LISTEN TO MY DECLARATION: WE HOLD THESE TRUTHS TO BE SELF-EVIDENT THAT ALL MEN ARE CREATED EQUAL . LOOK AROUND AT HOW LUCKY WE ARE TO BE ALIVE RIGHT NOW! HISTORY IS HAPPENING IN MANHATTAN AND WE JUST HAPPEN TO BE

IN THE GREATEST CITY IN THE WORLD!

JASMINE CEPHAS JONES

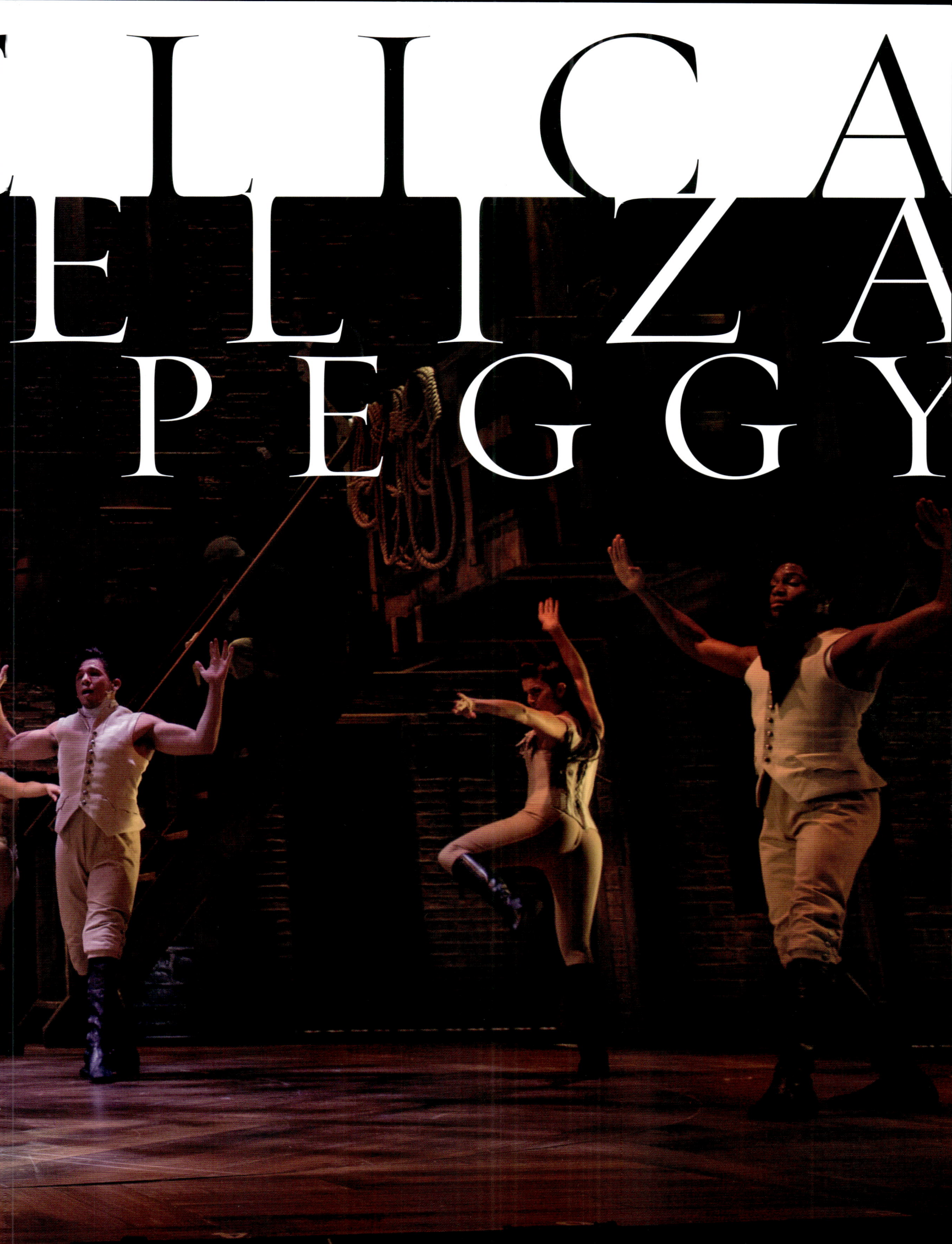

RENÉE ELISE GOLDSBERRY, LIN-MANUEL MIRANDA AND PHILLIPA SOO

M Y   S I

IF IT
TAKES
FIGHTING
A WAR
FOR US
TO MEET,
IT WILL
HAVE BEEN
WORTH IT.

STER

LIN-MANUEL MIRANDA
AND PHILLIPA SOO

I REMEMBER THAT
NIGHT, I JUST MIGHT
REGRET THAT NIGHT
FOR THE REST OF MY
DAYS,
I REMEMBER THOSE
SOLDIER BOYS
TRIPPING OVER
THEMSELVES TO WIN
OUR PRAISE.
I REMEMBER
THAT DREAMLIKE
CANDLELIGHT
LIKE A DREAM THAT
YOU CAN'T QUITE
PLACE,
BUT ALEXANDER, I'LL
NEVER FORGET THE
FIRST
TIME I SAW YOUR
FACE.
I HAVE NEVER BEEN
THE SAME,
INTELLIGENT EYES
IN A HUNGER-PANG
FRAME,
AND WHEN YOU SAID
"HI," I FORGOT MY
DANG NAME,
SET MY HEART
AFLAME, EV'RY PART
AFLAME.

CAN I BE REAL A SECOND? FOR JUST A
MILLISECOND? LET DOWN MY GUARD AND
TELL THE PEOPLE HOW I FEEL A SECOND?
NOW I'M THE MODEL OF A MODERN MAJOR
GENERAL, THE VENERATED VIRGINIAN
VETERAN WHOSE MEN ARE ALL LINING UP,
TO PUT ME UP ON A PEDASTAL, WRITIN'
LETTERS TO RELATIVES EMBELLISHIN'
MY ELEGANCE AND ELOQUENCE, BUT
THE ELEPHANT IS IN THE ROOM,
THE TRUTH IS IN YA FACE WHEN YA
HEAR THE BRITISH CANNONS GO...

BOOM

1776

OUI OUI, MON AMI, JE M'APPELLE LAFAYETTE! THE LANCELOT OF THE
REVOLUTIONARY SET! I CAME FROM AFAR JUST TO SAY "BONSOIR!" TELL
THE KING "CASSE TOI!" WHO'S THE BEST? C'EST MOI!

BRRRAH BRRAAAH! I AM HERCULES MULLIGAN,
UP IN IT, LOVIN' IT, YES I HEARD YA MOTHER SAID "COME AGAIN?"

POUR ME ANOTHER BREW, SON! LET'S RAISE A COUPLE MORE...

DAVEED DIGGS

TO THE

REVOL

LAFAYETTE
HERCULES
LAURENS

OKIERIETE ONAODOWAN, DAVEED DIGGS AND ANTHONY RAMOS

OKIERIETE ONAODOWAN, DAVEED DIGGS AND ANTHONY RAMOS

UTION

DATDADADAYADA!

DATDA

DATDA

DATDADA

Be&ck

DAYADA!
DATDADADAYA
DATDADADAYA
DADADADATDADATDADADADAYADA

JONATHAN GROFF

DADADADATDADA
ADADADADATDADA
ATDAYADA!

OUTRUN.

HIT 'EM QUICK, GET OUT FAST. STAY ALIVE 'TIL THIS HORROR SHOW IS PAST. WE'RE GONNA FLY A LOT OF FLAGS HALF-MAST.

OUTLAST.

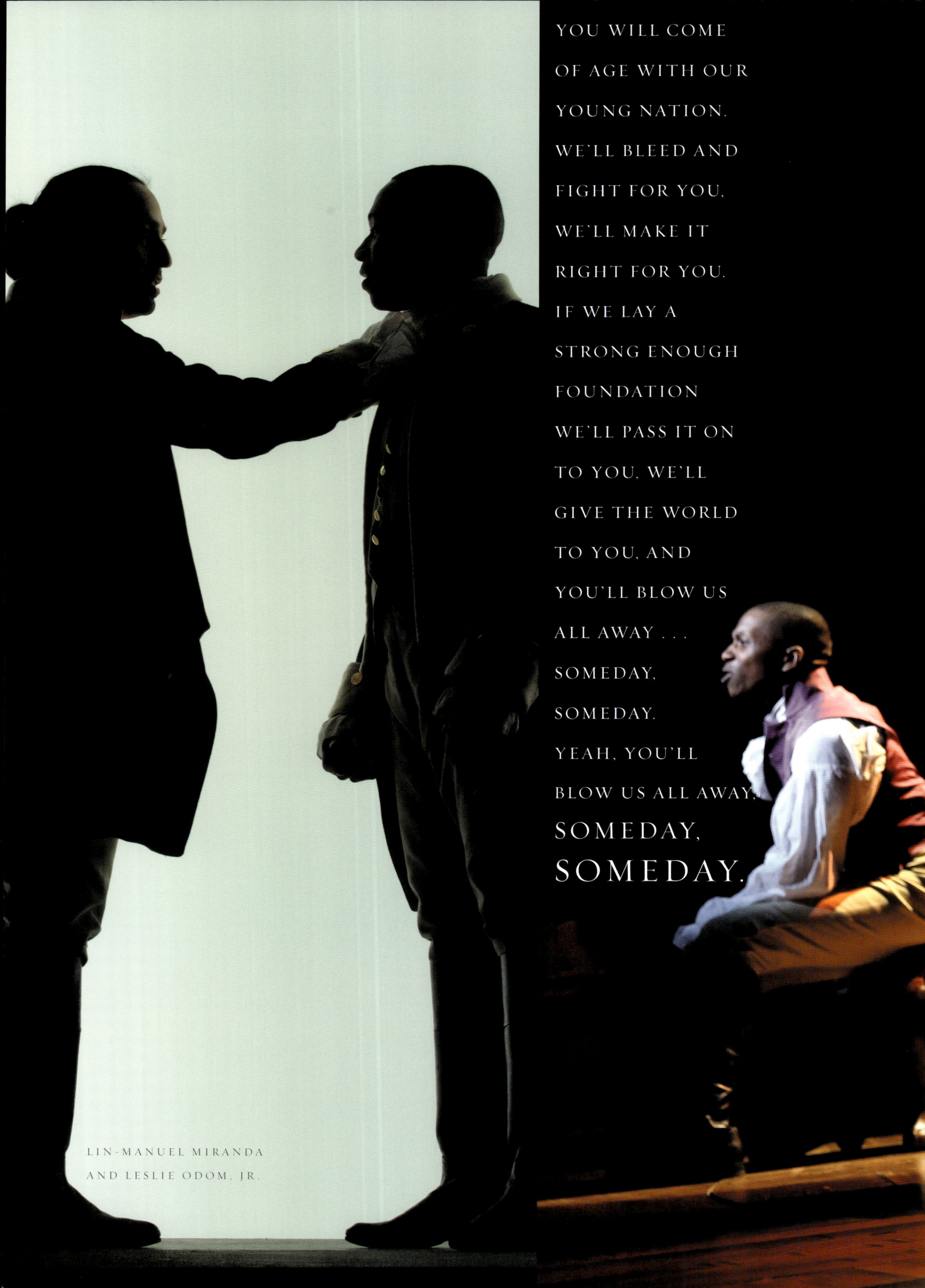

YOU WILL COME OF AGE WITH OUR YOUNG NATION. WE'LL BLEED AND FIGHT FOR YOU, WE'LL MAKE IT RIGHT FOR YOU. IF WE LAY A STRONG ENOUGH FOUNDATION WE'LL PASS IT ON TO YOU, WE'LL GIVE THE WORLD TO YOU, AND YOU'LL BLOW US ALL AWAY . . . SOMEDAY, SOMEDAY. YEAH, YOU'LL BLOW US ALL AWAY, SOMEDAY, SOMEDAY.

LIN-MANUEL MIRANDA AND LESLIE ODOM, JR.

LESLIE ODOM, JR. AND LIN-MANUEL MIRANDA

NUMBER ONE! THE CHALLENGE: DEMAND SATISFACTION. IF THEY APOLOGIZE, NO NEED FOR FURTHER ACTION. NUMBER TWO! IF THEY DON'T, GRAB A FRIEND, THAT'S YOUR SECOND. YOUR LIEUTENANT WHEN THERE'S RECKONING TO BE RECKONED. NUMBER THREE! HAVE YOUR SECONDS MEET FACE TO FACE. NEGOTIATE A PEACE… OR NEGOTIATE A TIME AND PLACE. THIS IS COMMONPLACE, 'SPECIALLY 'TWEEN RECRUITS. MOST DISPUTES DIE, AND NO ONE SHOOTS. NUMBER FOUR! IF THEY DON'T REACH A PEACE, THAT'S ALRIGHT. TIME TO GET SOME PISTOLS AND A DOCTOR ON SITE. YOU PAY HIM IN ADVANCE, YOU TREAT HIM WITH CIVILITY. YOU HAVE HIM TURN AROUND SO HE CAN HAVE DENIABILITY. FIVE! DUEL BEFORE THE SUN IS IN THE SKY. PICK A PLACE TO DIE WHERE IT'S HIGH AND DRY, NUMBER SIX! LEAVE A NOTE FOR YOUR NEXT OF KIN. TELL 'EM WHERE YOU BEEN. PRAY THAT HELL OR HEAVEN LETS YOU IN. SEVEN! CONFESS YOUR SINS, READY FOR THE MOMENT OF ADRENALINE WHEN YOU FINALLY FACE YOUR OPPONENT. NUMBER EIGHT! YOUR LAST CHANCE TO NEGOTIATE. SEND IN YOUR SECONDS, SEE IF THEY CAN SET THE RECORD STRAIGHT… NUMBER NINE! LOOK 'EM IN THE EYE, AIM NO HIGHER. SUMMON ALL THE COURAGE YOU REQUIRE. THEN COUNT ONE TWO THREE FOUR FIVE SIX SEVEN EIGHT NINE NUMBER TEN PACES!

FIRE!

THE TEN DUEL COM MAND MENTS

LIN-MANUEL MIRANDA

ANTHONY RAMOS AND EPHRAIM SYKES

JEF
FER
SON

SO WHAT'D I MISS?

DAVEED DIGGS

LADIES AND GENTLEMEN,
IN THE WORLD TONIGHT,
NEW YORK CITY.

YOU COULDA BEEN ANYWHERE
BUT YOU'RE HERE WITH US IN
ARE YOU READY FOR A CABINET MEETING???

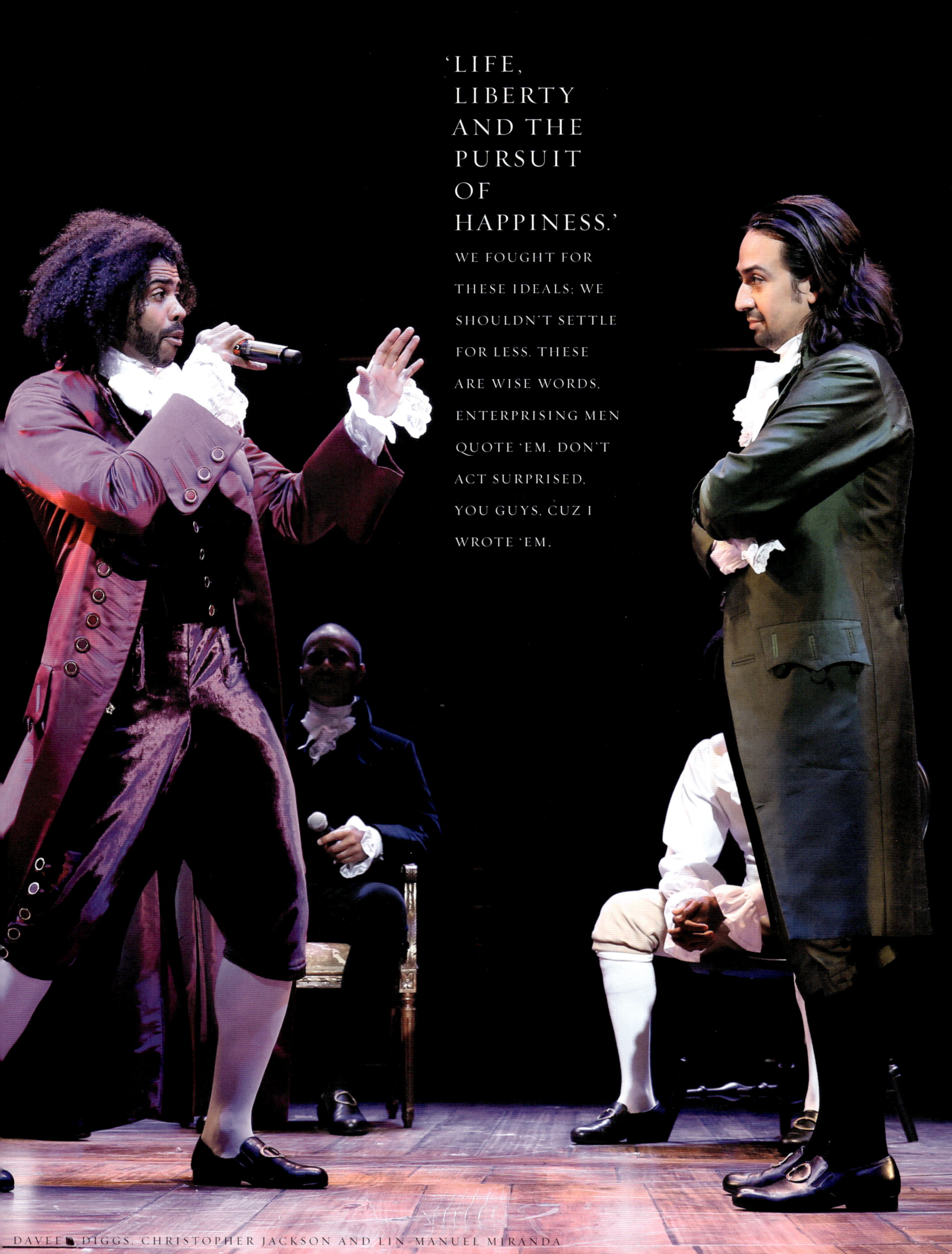

'LIFE, LIBERTY AND THE PURSUIT OF HAPPINESS.' WE FOUGHT FOR THESE IDEALS; WE SHOULDN'T SETTLE FOR LESS. THESE ARE WISE WORDS, ENTERPRISING MEN QUOTE 'EM. DON'T ACT SURPRISED, YOU GUYS, CUZ I WROTE 'EM.

DAVEED DIGGS, CHRISTOPHER JACKSON AND LIN-MANUEL MIRANDA

THOMAS. THAT WAS A REAL NICE DECLARATION. WELCOME TO THE PRESENT, WE'RE RUNNING A REAL NATION. WOULD YOU LIKE TO JOIN US, OR STAY MELLOW, DOIN' WHATEVER THE HELL IT IS YOU DO IN MONTICELLO?

ANGELICA & ELIZA WERE BOTH AT HIS SIDE WHEN HE DIED. DEATH DOESN'T DISCRIMINATE BETWEEN THE SINNERS AND THE SAINTS, IT TAKES AND IT TAKES AND IT TAKES. HISTORY OBLITERATES IN EVERY PICTURE IT PAINTS, IT PAINTS ME WITH ALL MY MISTAKES. WHEN ALEXANDER AIMED AT THE SKY, HE MAY HAVE BEEN THE FIRST ONE TO DIE, BUT I'M THE ONE WHO PAID FOR IT. I SURVIVED, BUT I PAID FOR IT. NOW I'M THE VILLAIN IN YOUR HISTORY. I WAS TOO YOUNG AND BLIND TO SEE... I SHOULD'VE KNOWN. I SHOULD'VE KNOWN THE WORLD WAS WIDE ENOUGH FOR BOTH HAMILTON AND ME.

A.

H

A

M

A.

B

U

R

R

A
Я
U
Я
Я

A
H
A
M

LESLIE ODOM, JR.

LESLIE ODOM, JR. AND LIN-MANUEL MIRANDA

LIN-MANUEL MIRANDA

WHO LIVES,

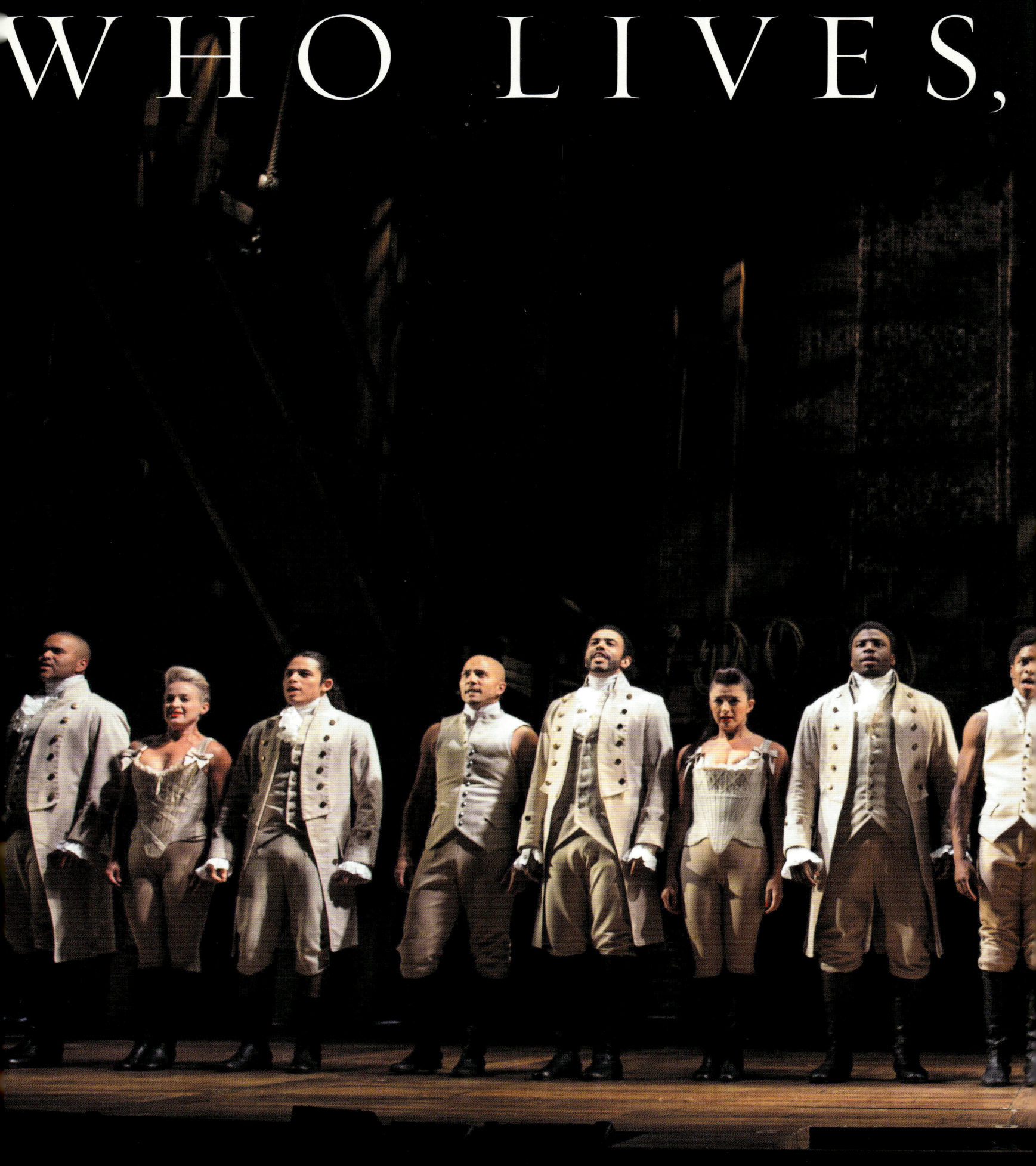

WHO TELLS

THOMAS KAIL
DIRECTOR

There is a spirit of generosity that Lin has stitched into the fabric of *Hamilton*. This spirit is evident in the stellar work of this company of performers. It is apparent in the carefully considered world the designers – David, Paul, Nevin and Howell – created. It is at the core of the work of our choreographer Andy's achievement. It is pulsing through the arrangements and orchestrations Alex gave us. It is, of course, mined from the source, Lin's words and music, which burst with a spirit of giving I have rarely seen.

The combination of this group and this material infuses a willing audience member with a feeling of possibility. Lin has wrought a show that does not merely demonstrate its intelligence and humanity, it invites all of us to participate in it. Lin, and the show, do not shout from far away, "Look at where we are," they build a bridge and make sure that everyone in the audience knows they are invited to join, and then show them how to join.

My job was to make sure we were all telling the same story and connect us to the impulse of generosity that first sparked in Lin when he decided to try and put his arms around this story. We worked hard, and we sure had fun along the way.

HOWELL BINKLEY
LIGHTING DESIGNER

The great thing, for me, about working on *Hamilton* has been the remarkable opportunity to spend my days in a room with such incredibly talented artists. I am thrilled to have been be a part of all of that; the layering of differing, brilliant craftspeople all in one space. I have been truly blessed to be surrounded by the best of the best in my beloved theatre on this piece and I learned from every single one of them.

Having said that, it is also quite daunting to have 50 songs put in front of us and accept the great challenge of making each look fresh with no repetition.

I have always believed my job is to sculpt around what a show has to say. An audience should not see the lights, they should see lives. I never want my work to overpower the book, music or the performances; I simply want to enhance them as much as possible. Therefore, our background work was of the utmost importance. We read, did a great deal of research and endlessly studied the script to discover every intricacy.

There was so much to play with here: the creations of my fellow artists and Lin's marriage of past and present. As a lighting designer, imagination has always been my favorite "gear," and our team was never once lacking. Being a part of *Hamilton* has truly been one of the best experiences of my career.

NEVIN STEINBERG
SOUND DESIGNER

I have never in my career been in a room where the stakes were so high, but the working temperature of the artistic collaboration stayed so low. It's a rare and wonderful thing to be a part of. Focus, credibility, comfort, trust and fierce ambition on full display, but with only the healthiest parts of everyone's ego in attendance. And, of course, joy. I will never forget the laughs. It reminded me of when I played high-school football and I'd wake up on Saturday morning to a blue sky, crisp autumn temperatures and only the slightest breeze – perfect playing conditions for game day – and enter the locker room with the utmost confidence in my coaches and teammates. Going to work on *Hamilton* was like that every day.

ALEX LACAMOIRE
MUSIC DIRECTOR, ORCHESTRATIONS, CO-ARRANGER

Have you ever tried to explain *Hamilton* to someone who doesn't know anything about the show? You know how they look at you when you say to them that it's about Founding Father Alexander Hamilton, but it's mostly hip-hop? Their minds can't quite picture how those things fit together, even though they acknowledge that it sounds interesting. My mind couldn't quite picture it either on the day that Lin explained his concept to me in my office at the Richard Rodgers Theatre while *In the Heights* was still running (the same office I have now, btw. There's no place like home). In that room, Lin showed me a five-chord sequence and asked me to play under him while he rapped the opening number. And then I understood what he meant. Not long after that, Lin and I were at the White House performing that same song for President Obama and the first lady. The minds of those in attendance didn't quite picture how those things fit together when Lin explained what he'd prepared for the evening ("You laugh, but it's true!" he cried). But then Lin started rapping, and they understood what he meant.

The thing is this: Lin's brain operates at an ultra-high level. Words are his gift — they come to him at breakneck speed and he's able to draw connections and create poetry with intense passion and profound meaning (kinda like Alexander Hamilton himself). So Lin was inspired by a biography, and it sparked something in him, and out came words and music unlike anything that has come before. As I like to say: we are all here because of some book Lin read.

My entire experience on *Hamilton* has been one that fills me with immense gratitude.

For starters, I get to be part of a dream team that Lin calls The Cabinet. Not only are Lin-Manuel Miranda / Tommy Kail / Andy Blankenbuehler the best composer/director/choreographer that I've ever worked with — they are also my friends. When the four of us get together to work, it's always a fluid and candid exchange of ideas that go back and forth, continuously inspiring one another until we land upon something that just "clicks" and would never have existed had it not been for the collaboration. The fact that these guys are so brilliant is intimidating, but it motivates me to bring my A-game every single time. If they like something that I've brought in, then it must be good.

I'm grateful that I get to sit in the best seat in the house, leading the best band I've ever assembled, playing in the pit of my favorite theater on Broadway, accompanying the most talented cast I've ever worked with.

I'm thankful for my music team and their endless support.

I love that the entire design team is so on point. When I watch the show, what strikes me is that every single department knocked it out of the park. The first time I got to see Korins' set with Howell's lights and Paul's costumes, I felt like everything was working together in perfect harmony. They shaped a world that was classy, retro AND modern at the same time, and in sync with the feel of the show. Once Nevin filtered all things sound through his crystalline design, we had a complete package, one that still stuns me.

I'm grateful for our producers and everyone who nurtured this piece, paving the road for us to get to where we are today.

I'm blessed with a wife who supported me every step of the way, forgiving me when I spent countless hours searching for the perfect phrase while staring at a computer screen instead of spending time with her. Thank you, Ileana.

Most of all, I'm grateful for Lin-Manuel Miranda. Aside from Lin's mind-boggling talent and quick wit and irresistible charm, he radiates a sense of inclusion in his work and in his being. He loves to play, and he loves to enlist people to join him in the sandbox. I feel honored that Lin has trusted me to be his right-hand man, allowing me to carry out his music and to put my own touches along the way. I once said to him: "All I ever want to do is create something that makes you go 'Woooooh!'" Again, if HE likes something that I brought in, then it must be good.

I have never poured so much of myself into a piece that gives back as much as I put into it. Sometimes you write and it feels labored, like you're not getting anywhere with your contribution. But *Hamilton* has always felt as if it's rewarding me for all the time I've spent working out vocal harmonies and recording demos and orchestrating strings, simply by allowing me to be a part of something special and unique, which is extremely fulfilling as an artist.

I felt that it was my duty to live up to the promise of Lin's work. We all felt like it was our duty. Tommy called it about two years before we even got to Broadway, before I even orchestrated a note. He said to me: "This is going to be your best work to date." I feel like I gave this piece my absolute best self, and I'm lucky that I get to share this with people.

I'm lucky that I live in a time when Lin-Manuel Miranda is composing for musical theater. (Look around, look around at how lucky we are to be alive right now.)

I'm lucky that I get to do what I love.

Most of all, I'm grateful.

ANDY BLANKENBUEHLER
CHOREOGRAPHER

About two years ago, I was sitting in a small rehearsal studio downtown listening to a table reading of *Hamilton*'s second act. That was the first time I heard "The Room Where It Happens." That song instantly became my favorite piece of music in the show. I knew the dance could be extraordinary, but every version I staged in workshops sorely disappointed me. We started rehearsals for the Public production. Again, I scrapped several more drafts, knowing that my work wasn't nearly living up to the goldmine that had been created by Lin-Manuel, Tommy and Alex.

Then one day, more than halfway through rehearsals, Lin added a new bridge to the music. I didn't have the answer of how to stage the song, and now I had another bridge to work into the mix. Time was running out. After a long day of rehearsal and dinner with my family, I went into the dance studio alone at about 9 p.m. It was winter. The studio was cold, and so I put on three layers of sweat pants and two sweatshirts.

In the scene, Burr wants to transport himself into a "room" where anything and everything is possible. I, too, have spent much of my life dreaming about possibilities. Feeling like they are out of reach is crushing, but then I was struck with the realization that I was no longer on the outside. Working on *Hamilton*, I was actually in the room that I had been dreaming about my entire life. As soon as I saw myself in the middle of the fantasy, I knew what to do. The dam burst open when I realized that I literally needed to build the room around myself.

First chorus: the room needed four corners. At *Hamilton*, those four corners are Lin-Manuel, Tommy Kail, Alex Lacamoire and my associate Stephanie Klemons. Burr would be in the middle of four dancers representing the corners of the room. I knew the moment needed to take root from a place of grounded simplicity. I used Bob Fosse as my inspiration in this section. The movement was tiny, flirtatious, but with laser focus.

Second chorus: we needed walls. I have never worked with an ensemble with more raw ability, polished refinement, or dedication than the dancers who would step forward to form the walls of this room. For me, they have become the walls that support a vision that I saw in my head, but which I could have never accomplished alone. The movement got more syncopated with some swagger borrowed from Justin Timberlake.

Third chorus: Jefferson, Madison and Hamilton sit at a luxurious table with drinks in their hands. Burr stands in the room, nearly exploding from the excitement of being in their presence. This is how I felt being in the room with the team of *Hamilton*. This is how I felt as a teenager discovering theater and dance. Into this chorus, I throw Fred Astaire, Gene Kelly, Dick Van Dyke and the Nicholas Brothers—voices that were part of my life when my excitement for dance took root.

I'm very proud of the final version of "The Room Where It Happens," but in truth, it never would have come to be if Lin-Manuel had not decided to write that new bridge. The bass haunts from underneath, and Hamilton says,

> "When you got skin in the game, you stay in the game.
> But you don't get a win unless you play in the game. Oh,
> you get love for it. You get hate for it. You get nothing
> if you wait for it. God help and forgive me, I wanna
> build something that's gonna outlive me. What do
> you want, Burr? If you stand for nothing, Burr, what
> do you fall for?"

Choreographing *Hamilton* is a once-in-a-lifetime gift. I had been given the opportunity to get in the trenches with the finest collaborators—all hungry and all working at the height of their abilities. As a creative artist, it's a scary and vulnerable thing to put yourself out there through your work. But like the soldiers fighting for their independence or the Founding Fathers battling to form their government, I believed with all my heart in what I was helping to create. I sweated through all those layers of clothing as I danced this section over and over again until it was perfect. It's my favorite moment.

With the bridge of the song behind me, the rest of the number spilled out. I pull from my idol Jerome Robbins, as the dancers show us the horizon line of possibilities. I have Susan Stroman on one shoulder and Christopher Chadman on the other, as the men clap and the tablecloth is pulled from beneath Burr's feet. We drive forward on Alex Lacamoire's powerhouse arrangements, as the cast brings to life how Andy Blankenbuehler feels about being on the Broadway boards with the show of a lifetime.

For me, *Hamilton* has been about taking everything I know about dance and crashing it together with everything that I know about life. I owe a lot to my idols. I am even more indebted to my family and friends. I finished in the studio at about 3 a.m., finally having found the dance that perhaps I love most in all of my career. What an absolute thrill to know that I really am in "The Room Where It Happens."

MILTON

JEFFERSON

HAMILTON

ELIZA

PAUL TAZEWELL
COSTUME DESIGNER

The first time that Tommy approached me, roughly two years ago, about working on *Hamilton*, it was still under the working title *Hamilton Mixtape*. My internal response was, "Huh? A musical about Alexander Hamilton?" I had never thought him to be a particularly dynamic figure in American history—not like George Washington or Paul Revere had been. I definitely did not imagine Hamilton's story as a sure thing to translate to the stage. However, my last project with both Tommy and Lin had been *In the Heights*, and it had been one of the few dream projects of my career. All of the right elements had been there. Lin, Tommy, and the creative team had been inspiring, infectious, genuine, humble, and passionate beyond measure. So when Tommy approached me about *Hamilton*, I was like, "I'm in!"

I may be stating the obvious, but design, or a chosen reduction of design, is essential to telling a story. Unless there is a clock on stage, sets, costumes, lights, and sound are needed to show the passage of years, the state of surroundings, and provide social strata. Creating a costume design vocabulary for *Hamilton* was like walking a tightrope. Push the clothes too far into the period vernacular and watch the show turn into a museum piece. Make them too anachronistic ("Hey, why is Hamilton wearing Nikes?"), and you lose the audience in a totally different fashion. What we were hoping for was a way to make these people on stage feel vital, immediate, and real without compromising the framework that Hamilton's life was providing the show. This approach was meant to focus on the cultural and racial honesty of the performers—an idea integral to the message of the piece.

One of the first decisions Tommy and I made was that the actors would be modern from the head up in terms of hair, makeup, etc. From the neck down, we would reference the period shapes from the different decades of the late 18th and early 19th century. I love the fabrics. I savor the detailing. I am in awe of these beautiful dresses and suits built almost entirely by hand. But, I knew that *Hamilton* was not that type of show. Lin's score, lyrics, and book deserved a strong but less distracting statement. This was not meant to be a fussy show. I was really inspired by the lyric "history is happening," as if we would be seeing the past and yet witnessing a dynamic new history being made simultaneously.

After initially meeting with Tommy, I laid out silhouettes (or line drawings) of a costume without any detail sketched in. Then I culled through hundreds of modern images of people, from rappers, to models, to skateboarders and the like, and looked for details that could have existed in both the 18th century and today. I used these details to flesh in those line drawings—adding and subtracting until it felt fresh and truthful. What I really wanted was for the clothes to somehow register as both bold and recessive in the same garment, to allow fluidity for the performers. The cast needed to to be dressed in a way that felt true to who they are as contemporary people as well as reflective of the 18th-century characters they were portraying. The opening has the company in neutral beige, cream, parchment—an almost spectral chorus. The actors would be able to tell the synopsis of the story to the audience as a uniform entity and later be differentiated, as their character(s) become more specific in the telling of the show. Only Burr, who from the very top is the narrator of sorts, wears a fully detailed and colored ensemble.

The fabrics I used are meant to keep the visual vocabulary streamlined. I chose the same types of fabrics (silk taffeta, cotton velvets, wool flannel, silk satin), avoided any obvious pattern, and kept a tightly controlled color palette. Hamilton's "treasury" green (a personal request from Lin), Jefferson's "bon vivant rockstar" look, and Maria's flame-colored dress break through that neutral wall into the world of bold color—but I think they are very successful at telling those characters' stories while staying true to the overall look of the costumes.

I personally feel that there is a certain school of thought which considers designing for Broadway to mean exaggeration, flash, oversized detailing, and dazzling mechanics. The costume designs for *Hamilton* might not match those particular views of design, instead relying more on a controlled, neutralized point of view that feels more akin to a Shakespearean play. I hope folks get something out of the stage pictures that are created with the costumes as they experience the universal story of Alexander Hamilton's life.

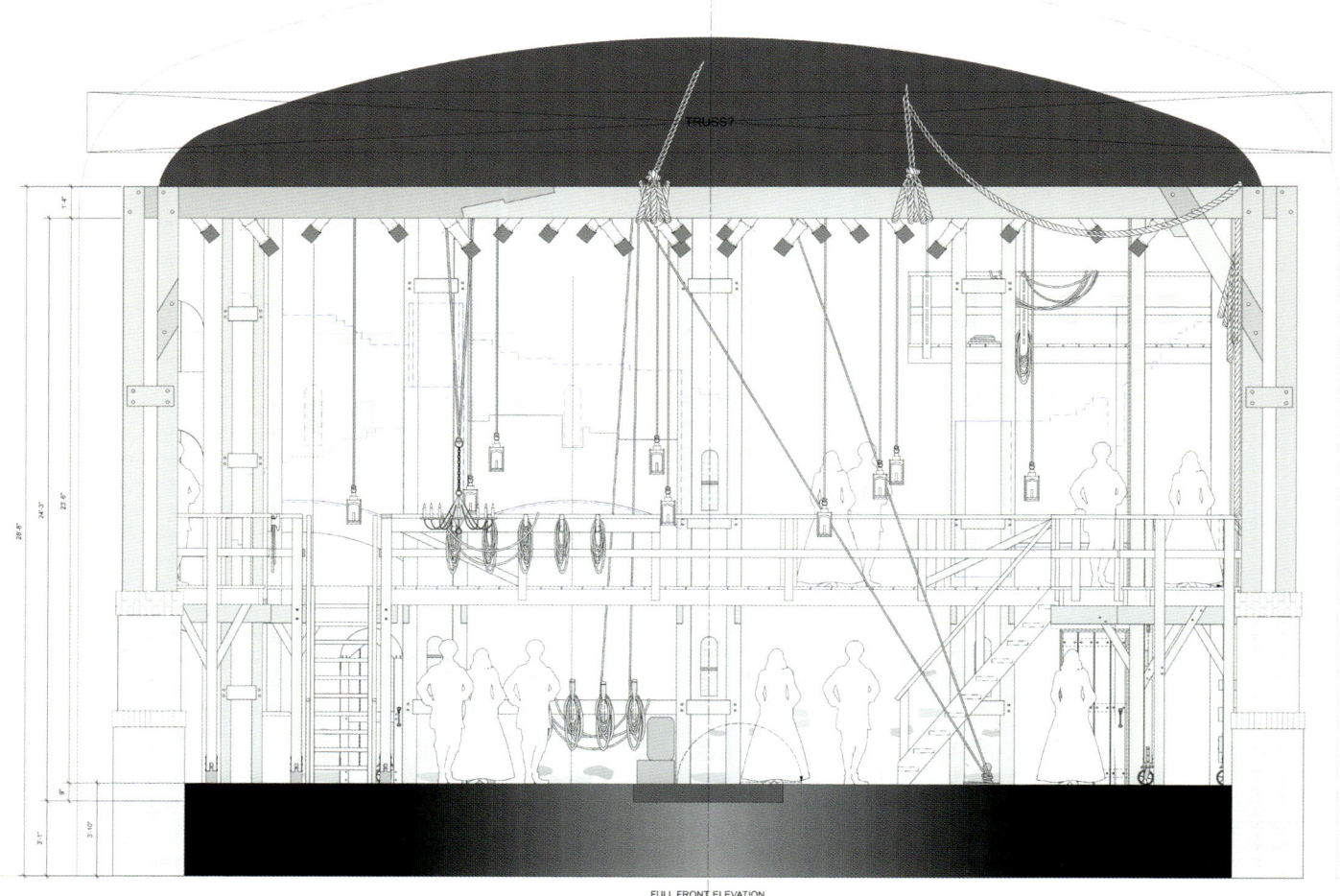

FULL FRONT ELEVATION
Scale: 1/2" = 1'-0"